THE PUPPY IN THE RED-CHECKERED COAT
Meets Santa

Written by
Amy Murphy & Rob Otto

Illustrated by
Diana Jacob

Amy Murphy

Rob Otto

We dedicate this book to Oscar,
the real puppy in the red-checkered coat.

Oscar

**The Puppy in the Red-Checkered Coat
Meets Santa**

Written by Amy Murphy & Rob Otto
Illustrated by Diana Jacob
Edited by Marla McKenna
Layout by Griffin Mill

ISBN: 978-1-957351-06-3

Published by Nico 11 Publishing & Design
Mukwonago, Wisconsin
www.nico11publishing.com
Michael Nicloy, Publisher

Be well read.

Quantity orders my be purchased directly from the publisher.
Send requests to: mike@nico11publishing.com

Printed in the United States of America

Hi, I'm Oscar, and I live with the greatest Mommy and Daddy ever. They are not really my mommy and daddy because they are people and I'm a puppy.

There is a lot of excitement going on right now.
Daddy brought a tree into the house,
and he's hanging his socks on the fireplace.
Mommy says she got an early Christmas present for me.
Come on, let's go see what it is!

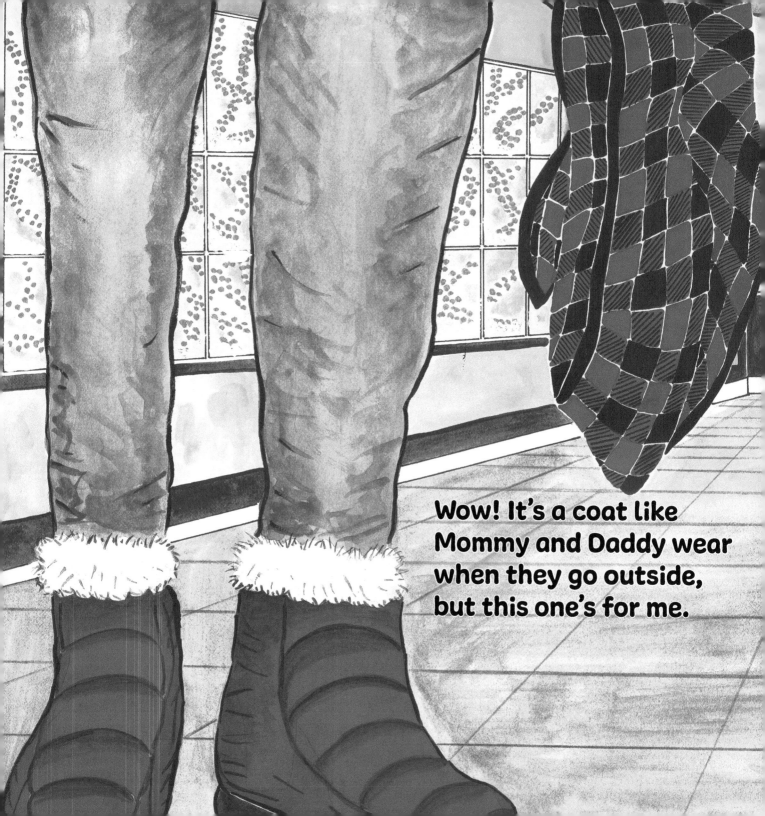

Wow! It's a coat like Mommy and Daddy wear when they go outside, but this one's for me.

It's red and black, and I bet it will keep me warm when I play in the cold, white stuff that falls from the sky. Oh boy, I can't wait to try it out!

Yippee, look at me running and playing
in my new red-checkered coat.
I LOVE IT!!
Daddy even has my leash!
Oh boy, we must be going for a walk!
Woof!
I wonder where we are going?

We must be downtown!
I like downtown because we walk
by the pond, and I get to bark at the
silly-looking birds!

Huh, downtown sure looks different today. There are sparkly lights on the trees and people everywhere singing and smiling. Something special must be going on...

Look, there's my friend Ivy! She is a puppy that lives down my street. Ivy is a little bit older than me.

Maybe she knows what all the fuss is about.
"Hey Ivy, do you know what's going on?" I asked.

"Oscar, don't you know? We're waiting to see Santa Claus in the Christmas Parade," replied Ivy.

"Sandy Claws? What's that?" I said.

"No, not sandy claws...Santa Claus," Ivy said with a woof. "He brings presents to all the good boys and girls, and puppy dogs too."

I know her! Daddy calls her the Mayor.
She's nice and smells good too.

Daddy says she has a key to give to Santa Claus.
I wonder if she has a treat for me too?

**What's that noise? I hear bells ringing.
What could be coming?**

I can't believe my eyes. Those are the **BIGGEST** dogs
I have ever seen. Their paws are funny looking and
their ears are big and pointy...I'm going to go say hello
and welcome them to my town.

Hey, look, what is around their necks?
They have collars with bells on them.

They must be the ones making that jingle bell noise. And they're pulling a big red sled. I wonder what is in there??

Who could that be? He's big and jolly and he has white fur on his chin. He even has a red coat like me (but he doesn't have checkers on his).
Did Mommy just call him Santa Claus? This must be SANDY CLAWS that Ivy told me about. Wow! Look at all those presents in his bag!
I hope there's a bone in there for me.

I'm glad we met.
He knows just the right
spot behind my ear to scratch.

I guess it's time to go home.

Bye Santa Claus.

Woof!

That was the most exciting walk <u>ever</u>!

I got to meet those BIG dogs pulling Sandy Claws in a sled, I barked at the geese, talked with my friend Ivy, and even jumped on the Mayor! (*Yawn*) I'm ready for bed.

I wonder if I'll see Santa Claus tonight...

"Merry Christmas, Puppy with the red-checkered coat."

~ The End ~

About the Authors and Illustrator

Amy Murphy

Amy has been writing since grade school and was inspired by her dog Oscar and his antics to write this story. Amy is married to Gregg and the mother of 7-year-old twins, McKenna and Brody, to whom she dedicates this book. Amy is a proud graduate of Central Michigan University, working in the communications field. She lives in Milford, Michigan, and is constantly inspired by her children and her pets, Olive, a black lab, and Butterscotch, a Manx cat.

Rob Otto

Rob has written for magazines, websites, role-playing games, and is working on selling his first film script. He is a former radio and television broadcaster and currently works for Winning Futures, a non-profit organization that mentors high school students in metro-Detroit. Rob is an honored graduate of Central Michigan University, and lives in Redford Township, Michigan.

Diana Jacob

Diana has been an art lover and art follower since childhood. She started out with painting landscapes, cityscapes, still life, nature, and various other subjects. Later she found herself drawn towards children's book illustrations because of their eye pleasing textures, colors, and cute character designs. Moreover, the enviable but daunting task of creating meaningful images that bring a children's book to life, appealed to her the most. She was born and brought up in India, where she still lives and works.

Oscar, a rescue pup from the humane society, attended the Brighton Holiday Glow where he jumped on the mayor, barked at reindeer, and met Santa Claus, or as he called him, Sandy Claws, all in his red-checkered coat. Oscar was a wonderful dog who was loved by many.

Scan here to follow the Puppy in the Red-Checkered Coat!

Printed in the USA
CPSIA information can be obtained
at www.ICGtesting.com
JSHW041124151123
51833JS00001B/4

* 9 7 8 1 9 5 7 3 5 1 0 6 3 *